IKE & MAMA
and the Once-in-a-Lifetime Movie

by CAROL SNYDER
drawings by CHARLES ROBINSON

Coward, McCann & Geoghegan, Inc., New York

To Patricia Lee Gauch
With thanks for sharing knowledge, enthusiasm and friendship

And in memory of
Eva Glasberg, my Grandmother,
and Ferdinand Monjo, editor and friend,
who introduced Ike and Mama to the children of today

Published simultaneously in Canada by Academic Press Canada Limited, Toronto.

Library of Congress Cataloging in Publication Data
Snyder, Carol.
Ike and Mama and the once-in-a-lifetime movie.
SUMMARY: Ike Greenberg and his friends appear as extras in a D. W. Griffith movie and surprise their families.
[1. Motion pictures—Fiction. 2. Jews in the United States—Fiction. 3. New York (City)—Fiction] I. Robinson, Charles, II. Title.
PZ7.S68517Im [Fic] 80-27374
ISBN 0-698-20501-4

First printing
Designed by Catherine Stock
Printed in the United States of America

Contents

1. The Boys in a Hurry

"Mama!" Ike stood on the sidewalk, looked up and shouted. The third-floor window was partly open, and he could see Mama in the kitchen.

"Please, Mama," he called again, "cut me off, *shmear* me over, throw me down from the window a piece of bread and butter." Ike's singsong voice rippled through the frosty March air. "I'm ready to leave," he added.

The window opened farther with a bang and a screech, and Mama stuck her head out.

"You want also an apple?" Mama asked. "So here." She reached out the window and dropped a brown paper bag from her fingertips. "You share with the others," she called.

Ike's cousins Sammy and Dave, and his friends Tony Golida and tall Danny Mantussi from downstairs, crowded around Ike, watching the bulging bag speed down three floors. Ike positioned himself to catch it as if he were an outfielder in a baseball game at the Polo Grounds. It landed right smack in his hands.

"I already have three cents," Ike shouted, patting his pocket.

"You find someone else with two cents, Ikey," Mama said, waving her finger in warning. "You pay the bargain ticket price, two for a nickel, and walk into the movie house like a gentleman. You are not to sneak into the movies. You hear? Sneaking in would be cheating the theater man. He has to make a living, too."

On Ike's block, East 136th Street in the Bronx, no one had five cents to spend on the movies, but on bargain day, two for a nickel, all the kids went.

"And my head is cold, Ikey," Mama added. "So put on your cap."

From the bottom step, Ike picked up his woolen cap and arranged it on top of his curly hair.

Mama started to pull herself back inside but

stopped and added, "And take Bessie with you. Under five years is no charge if she sits on your lap."

"But Mama!" Ike said no more because the window slammed shut.

He felt like a balloon with the air let out. Going to the movie matinee was his favorite thing to do but not with his little sister Bessie tagging along. This would be Bessie's first time at the movies. She might be afraid of the dark, Ike thought. She might even cry! None of the other boys had to take their sisters. It wasn't fair. And she'd probably tell Mama everything when they got back, everything the boys did. But how could Ike complain? At least Mama was letting him go to the movies, even though it was the Sabbath—a day Mama herself would never go. "We are in America," she'd reasoned to Papa. "I cannot say no to everything, not in the Bronx, or Ikey will just learn to say no to me and to God. So today he must go with his friends."

"Hurry, Ike!" Tony pulled at Ike's jacket. "We don't want to miss even the newsreel."

There was always something interesting in the Pathé News film these days. So far, 1920 was a happy year with the war over and the soldiers back and talk about women voting. Ike especially liked the beginning of the news when the big rooster squawked and they showed the man with the movie camera. Movies were as magical as Houdini. From nowhere people could appear and disappear on the big screen. And the lines of words silently telling the story trailed across the screen and changed to different words as the projector whirred in the high booth.

Tony Golida and Danny Mantussi were already headed down the street, limping along with one foot in the gutter and one on the sidewalk. Sammy and Dave jumped over the stair railing and followed. Ike grabbed Bessie who was pulling a cigar box by a string. In the box was a doll covered with newspapers.

"C'mon, we're going to the movies," he said, as he dragged her by the hand.

The third floor window opened again. Out came Mama's head.

"Ikey, wagons are for pulling. Sisters are for taking. And Bessie, my hands are cold, so put on your mittens from your pocket."

"Okay, Mama." Bessie waved.

"So have a good time, *kinder,* and remember everything so you'll tell me the story later."

The window slammed shut and the boys and Bessie dashed down the street. Morton Weinstein and James Higgins jumped down the steps and raced after them. And Jack, Robert and Patrick Murphy called from their stoop. They tossed their pennies, and Patrick said, "I've got two cents. Who's got three cents?" But Ike didn't hear him.

At the next apartment house, Joey, Bernie and Sol joined the ever-increasing army, and Herbie Friedman caught up with them near the corner. He was wheeling a wicker baby buggy.

"I can't go," Herbie muttered.

"Bring your baby sister along," Ike said, pulling Bessie.

Herbie explained that the problem was not his baby sister. He could get a number and park her in the lobby with the other babies in carriages. No. The problem was much worse than that. The problem was that his two cents were lost forever down the sewer.

"You can't even *see* them down there," he groaned.

"Gee," Ike said, making a clicking sound with his tongue, a sound Mama made when she felt sorry for someone.

The boys huddled together and whispered. They couldn't go to the movies and leave out a friend. But no matter how they figured, there was no money left for Herbie. A plan was needed. A plan to get Herbie into the movies without money.

An idea flashed through Ike's mind: a way to sneak

Herbie into the movie house. "Come with us anyway, Herbie," Ike said. "We'll think of something." It must be right to help a friend, he reasoned. But as he looked at Bessie he remembered Mama's words. "Tell me everything later," she'd said. Well, maybe Bessie wouldn't notice "everything." Ike hoped.

Then the East 136th Street "army" marched past the grocery store, the Chinese laundry and the butcher shop to the Osceola Theatre on East 138th Street and St. Anne's Avenue. The frosty air outside the movie house vibrated with the excitement of shivering, screaming and pushing boys and girls lining up in front of the ticket booth.

"I've got two cents. Who's got three cents?" they shouted.

Overhead the marquee was missing a letter "R," and Ike read the name of the movie out loud. "*B oken Blossoms,*" he said, and laughed.

Ike pulled Bessie, who pulled her cigar box. "I got three cents," he called and Patrick Murphy, smiling and tossing two pennies, got in line next to him.

Ike leaned against an easel with a poster of the beautiful movie star Lillian Gish and sniffed the air. The tantalizing smell of baked yams steamed from the nearby wagon.

James, Robert, Bernie, Sol and the others were

still dashing around mixing and matching into pairs that would add up to five cents each. In the flurry of activity, only Herbie stood motionless, holding on to the baby buggy. Ike called Herbie over and whispered his plan to him. Herbie disappeared around the side of the brick building, leaving the wicker baby carriage with Ike.

"Now you got a baby, too, Ikey." Bessie smiled up at her brother.

Ike didn't answer. He just put his bag of food under his arm, pushed the carriage and pulled Bessie as the line moved toward the ticket booth.

All the boys were on line now except for Herbie. Ike whispered the plan to Patrick, adding the words, "pass it on." Patrick turned and whispered the plan to Robert and Robert whispered to Jack. The secret plan to sneak Herbie in was passed on and on and on.

But, by the time the plan reached Tony, at the end of the line, something had been added. Something Ike had *not* planned. For as the boys had passed it on, the movie matinee help-your-friend plan had grown. To Ike's surprise, Tony ran up to him and whispered the enlarged plan. Then Tony, Sammy, Dave and tall Danny Mantussi walked around the brick building and joined Herbie in the alley. Ikey and the others still in line moved closer to the ticket booth.

The plan would take perfect timing, caution and quick thinking. For now the idea was to get not *one* but *five* friends into the Osceola Theatre without paying. Then with the money saved they would buy and share a box of Cracker Jack and a box of chocolate bonbons, which cost five cents each.

Ike waited for the line to move again. He shifted his weight from one foot to the other and he waited, wiggled and worried. As usual, Mama was waiting to hear about the movie so she could cry at the sad parts. But if Bessie found out the plan for helping friends, Mama would hear much more than just the story of *Broken Blossoms.* And worse yet, Ike knew he'd hear quite a story from Mama, and the tears might be his own.

He convinced himself that he wasn't actually *not* listening to Mama. "Pay your nickel," she'd said and he was paying. He *was* walking in like a gentleman, too; like Mama had said. And *he* was not sneaking in.

But he had to help his friends Herbie, Danny, Tony, Sammy and Dave sneak into the Osceola Theatre. Ike and the others planned to be seated inside, just three feet away from a steel fire door. Ike had told Herbie the signal: one knock on the fire door, then two softer knocks. He was sure he'd know just when to open the fire door for Herbie and the others. Things were going so easily today, Ike reminded himself, so, of course they'd never get caught.

Now Ike and Bessie were next in line. A woman wearing a stocking hat and gloves which smelled like a horse peered out the opening of the glass-windowed booth.

"Two for a nickel, one under five and I need a number for the baby carriage," Ike said, looking around nervously as he handed her the money. He tried to look everywhere but at the alley where five boys were waiting to sneak inside.

Bessie tugged at Ike's baggy knickers. "I need a number for my carriage, too," she said.

Ike gave her a disgusted look, but since this was the first time Bessie was at a movie, he patiently explained. "Cigar boxes don't need numbers. Dolls don't cry, Bessie. They put a number so if the baby in that carriage cries, they show that number on the screen inside. Letters spell out the words, 'Baby number four is crying,' and the mother goes to check on it."

"My baby may cry, too," Bessie said. "And I need

a number!" She squinted her eyes and Ike knew that meant business. "And where are the other b—"

Ike clamped his hand over her mouth and looked around hoping no one had heard her. He didn't want to stand out like an orange in a potato bin. Not with five friends waiting to be sneaked in the fire door.

"Okay, Bessie, shush already. Look on the ground. You have to find a number."

Ike took his ticket and a cardboard number six and thanked the woman. He pushed the carriage into the lobby. "What a pest," he mumbled as he helped Bessie search the lobby floor until they found an old discarded number four in a crushed Cracker Jack box.

While Bessie arranged the number four, her doll and her cigar-box buggy, Ike hung the number six on Herbie's sister's carriage and peeked inside. She was sound asleep. "Take good care of her," he said to the ticket woman, who was now in the lobby checking to see which babies were crying.

Bessie pointed to her cigar box. "Check my baby, too," she said.

The woman smiled.

Inside the crowded theater, four hundred people arranged themselves in the three sections. Ike removed his jacket and Bessie's, piled them up and sat

NOW PLAYING

on them in a seat up front and to the side, three feet from the fire door. He tried not to look at it. Jack, Patrick, Robert, Joey, Bernie, Sol, Morton and James did the same with their jackets and sat on them in the seats next to Ike. Bessie, not permitted to have a seat of her own, climbed into Ike's lap and rubbed the red velvet on the seat.

Ike and the other boys waited for the signal from outside the door. Any moment they would hear one knock, then two softer knocks. Ike hoped no one else would hear. Of course they wouldn't, he told himself. Not with all these noisy kids.

As the light bulbs on the sides of the theater went out, the children wiggled, sitting on top of their bulky jackets. Then the piano player struck a chord and the movie projector whirred.

At first Bessie was frightened by the darkness. She hugged Ike tightly, but at least she didn't cry. As Ike watched the screen and listened for the signal, the smell of an orange being peeled nearby made him swallow. Bessie looked at the screen and slapped her cheek in surprise as words appeared, but she could not read.

" 'Ladies . . . please remove hats.' " Ike whispered the caption to her. Morton Weinstein told the girl in front to please remove her head, and the other boys laughed. Cries of "Down in front, down in front," could be heard from boys and girls stretching to see. Mothers shushed from the back row.

When the Pathé News started, Bessie giggled at the sight of the rooster, and Ike almost missed his favorite part, the picture of the movie camera. He was busy glancing at the fire door and listening for the signal. Bessie snuggled in Ike's lap, relaxed now, and delighted. But Ike could not relax.

He knew he'd hear the signal any minute. His stomach felt like the time he ate a raw clam at Coney Island: unkosher, uncooked, uncomfortable. Then he heard it. . . .

A soft knock on the door. One knock—then two little ones. Ike poked Morton, who poked James, who poked Bernie, and the boys went into action. But so did the usher.

2. The Boys in Action

The movie projector whirred and lit up a beam of dust specks all the way from the booth to the screen. The usher headed for the fire door, following the ray of his flashlight. Had the usher heard the signal? One knock, then two more. Ike wished he could send an SOS through the heavy steel door: run Herbie, run Danny and Sammy, Tony and Dave. His heart pounded and his hands felt sweaty.

Please don't knock again, Ike thought—hard. The usher was almost at the door. Ike wished he could send messages like Houdini, through air and walls and everything. Maybe he had. All was quiet. The usher leaned against the wall next to the fire door, arms folded, and watched the Pathé News. Maybe the usher hadn't even heard the signal, Ike reassured himself, and tried to relax.

The picture showed a man with a wide-brimmed hat, a crooked nose and laughing eyes, ordering about people with cameras. Ike barely had time to whisper all the captions because after each sentence he glanced at the door.

" 'Movie industry returns to New York!

" 'Famous moviemaker D. W. Griffith forsakes Hollywood for Mamaroneck,' " Ike read quietly—and glanced at the door. " 'The new Griffith movie, *Way Down East,* is now being filmed on Griffith's Mamaroneck estate just north of the Bronx,' " he finished, breathlessly.

When Ike heard another knock, he knew he had to distract the usher, still leaning near the fire door only three feet away. Ike knew he had to make some noise.

"Just north of the Bronx!" Ike said out loud. Sitting up straight, almost knocking Bessie off his lap, Ike bellowed, "Real cameras! Just north of the Bronx!"

"*Sh,*" said the usher, pointing at Ike in the darkness. But he didn't move away from the fire door.

The next newsreel picture showed Mr. Griffith and the movie star Lillian Gish and a lot of other people of different ages, waiting around.

Ike glanced at the door. He pictured the five boys waiting restlessly outside. Don't knock! Ike sent another thought message. He coughed, hoping the usher would come toward him through the darkness and ask if he wanted some water.

Then the boys could sneak in.

The picture changed to captions, and after a kick from Bessie who said, "*READ,*" Ike read, coughing between words.

" 'People gather to watch the filming, [cough] hopeful for the chance to be an extra and earn a moment of fame, [cough, cough] and a dollar-fifty a day.' "

Now the other boys caught on to the coughing plan. At the end of the row Bernie coughed, then Morton, then James. But the usher still did not move from the fire door, just three feet away from Ike and Bessie. So the boys stopped coughing and listened some more.

"A dollar-fifty a day," Ike repeated to Morton as the words trailed off the screen. "So much money."

Bessie kicked again, and Ike read the captions as fast as he could.

" 'Griffith waits for a needed snowfall in this unusually snowless winter.' "

For a moment—like Mr. Griffith—Ike, too, thought about snow. The boys had been waiting for a good snowfall for months, but there had been none. No sliding down the hill on garbage-can covers. No snow cones to pour syrup over and lick. And no East 136th Street snowball fight.

With the interesting part about moviemakers and cameras over, Ike stopped watching the news and watched the door instead. Then Ike heard the one knock and two soft knocks. Of course Bessie also heard them.

"Someone's at the door," she announced in a loud voice.

He had to act fast. The usher was turning to the fire door. Ike knew he had to do something to get the usher away from the door and to keep Bessie quiet. So Ike reached into the brown bag, pulled out a piece of bread *shmeered* with butter and sugar and stuffed it into Bessie's mouth saying, "I'm hungry, Bessie, so eat something." And don't talk about the door, he thought.

He rattled the bag noisily, talked loudly and kicked the seat in front of him, making a sound of one knock, then two more.

This time the usher did move from the fire door. He pointed a finger at Ike. "*SH!*" he said again ". . . or else!" and he pointed toward the back.

Ike, squinting in the darkness, looked at Morton and shrugged his shoulders. Poor Herbie and Danny and Sammy and Dave. Poor Tony. They must be freezing out there in the alley. The movie matinee help-your-friend plan was taking a very long time. Every time Ike looked up, the usher was watching him. Ike took a bite of bread and passed some to his friends. He licked the creamy butter off his lips and wiped his sugary mouth on his sleeve.

"Sleeves are for wearing, hankies are for wiping," Bessie said, sounding like Mama.

This I needed today? Ike thought. A pesky, bossy sister?

This time there was no missing the knocks. They were not soft. They were impatient, loud knocks. And this time the usher reached for the steel bar on the door. They'd be caught for sure. The boys slid down in their seats as the usher started to open the door. It would be too painful to watch their friends' faces when they saw it was the usher letting them in and not Ike. If only they could do something.

Just then, Bessie jumped up and down and pointed to the screen where the movie, *Broken Blossoms,* was now on. Across the screen was a number four and the words: BABY #4 IS CRYING.

"What does it say about number four, Ikey, what?" she said loudly, for although she could not read, Bessie already knew lots of numbers from helping Mama sell cloth.

" 'Baby number four is crying,' it says," Ike muttered, peeking at the usher, who was about to open the door. Before Ike had a chance to explain that there was also a real baby number four, that Bessie had an old discarded ticket on her doll's cigar-box buggy, Bessie leaped up. Now she was right next to the usher. She grabbed the usher's red jacket and tugged at it. His hand slipped off the door handle as he whirled around to see who had attacked him. He saw no one until he looked down.

Bessie slipped her hand in his, yelling, "Baby number four is crying. I have to pick her up. Take me!" she ordered, and dragged him up the aisle.

So, like Mama says, Ike thought, "From bad luck, *tsuris,* sometimes comes something good." Whoever thought Bessie would help?

Quick as a speeding El train, Ike and the boys were in action. Ike crept over to the door and pushed the bar handle. The door opened fast, and light flashed in just for a second, before Ike, Morton and

James quickly closed it again. A shivering Herbie crawled along the floor, followed by frozen-nosed Sammy and Dave. Then came red-eared Danny and Tony Golida, all squinting away darkness, feeling their way up the row of seats along the dusty floor and over crushed Cracker Jack boxes and crinkly candy wrappers.

Bessie returned to the seat and climbed back onto Ike's lap. She dangled her feet and looked, not at the screen, where scenes from *Broken Blossoms* matched the piano player's villain music, but at the creeping boys.

"What are you looking for . . . a number? A ticket? What?" Bessie asked, remembering the search for the number four. She hopped off the seat, blocking the way. "What did you lose, Danny, a penny maybe?" she said, and she bent down to look.

"*Shh! Shh!*" said the woman in the next row. "And stop moving around like a cockroach."

"Shud up!" said the boy in the seat behind her.

"I'm looking for a seat," Danny muttered.

"On the floor?" Bessie asked loudly. "And where were you anyway?" she added.

The usher also had returned and was coming to see what the commotion was. Now Ike was certain they'd be caught. But just then, the entire audience

EXIT

started to boo, throw pieces of popcorn and stamp their feet.

The worst thing that could happen at a matinee had happened. The screen was black. "This movie should be called *Broken Film* instead of *Broken Blossoms,*" a girl called out.

While the usher was scurrying to the projection booth to see how long it would be until the film was fixed, all the boys quickly found seats in this row or that. Safe for sure, Ike thought.

Bessie tugged at Ike's sleeve, "My baby number four is sleeping again, in her buggy. It was all right to go with the policeman," she jabbered. "Mama said, 'Policemen are for helping.' "

"That's an usher, Bessie, not a policeman," Ike answered, looking around and feeling nervous at the mere mention of the word usher. For the usher was returning once again.

"What's an usher, Ikey?" Bessie asked.

"It's a high school boy who shines a skinny flashlight on empty seats and noisy kids." Ike thought that would keep Bessie still. But instead, much to his horror, she started waving to the usher and pointing to a noisy kid in the next row.

Ike pulled Bessie's arm. He had to think of a way to keep her quiet—and quickly.

"And Bessie," Ike said, "the usher is also . . . a stranger." He pronounced the serious word carefully.

"A stranger?" Bessie opened her blue eyes as far as she could. "Ikey," she whispered, "I went with a *stranger?*" She covered her mouth with her hand. "Don't tell Mama," she muttered.

Going with a stranger was something Mama warned against every day. It was the worst thing you could do.

"And you mustn't talk to strangers," Ike added. Now he knew Bessie would not wave to the usher, and maybe now she wouldn't tell Mama everything.

Then suddenly everyone was squinting at the brightness as the lights went on. As if it were intermission, the candyman, wearing his white long-sleeved coat and white peaked hat, began to hawk boxes of candy. He reached into the big box that hung from a strap around his neck and he held up a package of bonbons. In his other hand he waved a tin watch the way Mr. Klinger, the butcher, waves chickens.

"Buy a box of candy and get a free watch," the candy butcher bellowed.

"They only put watches in about ten boxes," Ike said, glancing around.

"CRACKER JACK!" the candyman sang, getting

everyone's attention. "With an earring or a whistle or a genuine fake diamond ring," he called. "Adjustable," he added, for effect.

"A ring?" Bessie looked up at Ike. Her eyes pleaded.

Ike was feeling relieved, now that the help-your-friend plan had worked. "Since my sister Bessie saved us by grabbing the usher," Ike whispered to his friends, "let's spend the other nickel for Cracker Jack and give her the prize." There was something about giving Bessie a present that delighted him. He was glad all the boys agreed, and, as he handed her the box, Ike hoped the prize was a ring.

Bessie happily ripped open the box and gave out handfuls of Cracker Jack. She searched for the prize, her hands sticky as a Friday night honey cake.

When a smell like naphtha soap and lilacs filled the air, Ike knew the usher must be in the aisle nearby, squirting his spray gun of disinfectant into each row, erasing leftover odors of sandwiches and fruit. "P.U.," Ike said, holding his nose. It smells like trouble, he thought. Maybe they were not safe after all.

As the usher came closer, he reached over and touched a boy's ear. Ike caught on too late. Too late to warn his friends, to tell them to rub their ears.

Five minutes inside had not removed all the March chill. The boys' faces were pale with fright, but a small part of their ears was still red and cold from their long wait outside.

Now the usher reached out and felt Danny's and Tony's ears. "Your ears are not all warmed up," he said. "You're the boys who sneaked in!"

Danny and Tony dug in their pockets as if they had late checks, tickets that showed they came late and could stay late. But, of course, they had none.

Then the usher recognized Ike. When he grabbed Ike, not to feel his ears, but to throw him, along with the other boys, out on their ears, that usher was in for a surprise.

For Bessie, who had found the prize at the bottom of the Cracker Jack box, used it. And it was not a ring, it was a whistle.

Bessie blew the whistle loudly and kicked the usher in the leg, yelling, "You let go of my brother! You *STRANGER!*"

What else could the boys do? A kicked usher could not be reasoned with. They grabbed their jackets, and Ike, pulling Bessie away from the usher, shouted, "We'll pay double next time," as they all dashed up the aisle to the lobby. Herbie grabbed his Baby #6 and Bessie tugged the string on her Baby #4's cigar box. Then they raced breathlessly out the front door, struggling only a moment to get the carriage through.

As the escaping army headed for East 136th Street, Ike yelled, "Button your coat, Bessie, I'm cold."

But what made him colder yet, was the thought of Mama—waiting to be told "everything."

3. Mama in Action

The boys, still running from the angry usher, were breathless as they raced past the butcher shop, the Chinese laundry and the grocery store. Danny Mantussi had to turn back to catch his cap as it flew off in the breeze, and Herbie's baby sister laughed out loud as the wicker carriage bumped and joggled, its wooden wheels spinning along the cement sidewalk. The smell of sour pickles from the barrel in front of the East 136th Street grocery store made Ike's mouth water as he stopped to pick up Bessie's cigar-box baby carriage before it fell apart.

"Boy, did I give a kick to that stranger!" Bessie panted, trying to catch her breath. "Just like Mama said. 'A stranger grabs you, you give a kick and run!' So now I listened to Mama. Right Ikey? You won't say I was bad?"

"Right," Ike muttered, not paying too much attention. The chilling thought of explaining to Mama about kicks and strangers and running from ushers and sneaking into the movies, for the first time made him dizzy. He slowed down.

Then, as the army reached Ike's red brick building, one by one the boys collapsed. Some gasped for air, others clutched their hearts or stomachs as they swarmed over the stoop, sitting on the cold steps or hanging over the iron railing, deciding if maybe today they *shouldn't* go up to Ike's apartment.

Their bottoms had barely touched the stairs when the window squealed open above, and Mama stuck her head out.

"You're back already? Some bargain-half price for half a movie? So, come up. I'm waiting to cry at the story. I'm waiting with apples and honey for you." Mama loved sad movies. According to Mama, if a movie couldn't make you cry, what good was it?

What could they do? They had to go up. Besides, who could resist apples and honey?

Ike opened the heavy front door for Bessie. Herbie lifted his baby sister out of the carriage and *shlepped* her up the stairs under his arm like the wet-wash man carries the laundry. Ike parked the wicker carriage under the stairs next to his bicycle. If it was left outside unattended the wooden wheels would surely be removed for use on some kid's homemade racing wagon. Bessie made Ike park her cigar-box buggy, too. She grabbed Baby #4, tucking the doll under her arm.

The smell of frying onions filled the hall. The boys' footsteps echoed loudly, but today they did not race up the three flights of stairs. Everyone walked slowly. After sneaking into the movies, they were in no hurry to look into Mama's eyes. Today they were in no hurry to tell Mama everything.

On the one hand, Ike was glad it was the Sabbath and Papa was still praying at the *shul.* But on the other hand, Ike felt a shiver go through him. Not only had he done something bad, but he had done it on Saturday, the Jewish Sabbath, yet. Would lightning strike him?

Now, as the boys crowded into the kitchen, Ike smelled the meaty smell of cholent still simmering from yesterday in the oven of the coal stove. The meat, bean and barley mixture cooked slowly by itself requiring no work on the Sabbath, and heating the kitchen.

Mama sat by the window with a big bowl of apples in front of her on the table.

"I'm hot from the oven," Mama said, shaking the white collar of her blouse. "So take off your jackets, *kinder.*" Then she pointed to the apples. "And Danny darling, on the Sabbath I cannot peel since that would be like working. So today you will peel the apples for us?" Mama pointed to the knife on the table.

Danny Mantussi, pleased to be chosen by Mama, started peeling and slicing the apples, piling long curls of apple peel on yesterday's *Daily Forward* newspaper as Mama instructed.

Mama looked up at Ike, who peered in from the doorway. "Come here, Ikey," she said. "What is wrong? You're as pale as these peeled apples." She put her lips to his forehead. "You're sick? You have a fever maybe? That's why you're home so early?"

Ike wished he did have a fever. How simple that would be. Mama would put a wet cloth over his forehead, and he might be too sick to tell about sneaking into the movies.

"No," Mama said, "you are as cool as a cucumber. So eat a something. I'm hungry."

The boys took off their jackets and stacked them on a chair. Then they munched apples dipped in thick honey. Ike was glad their mouths were busy with food, not talk. Honey dripped down James Higgins' chin and he licked it off.

Mama reached for Herbie's baby sister and made loud kissing noises murmuring, "*Shayner maideleh,* a real heart breaker this one will be, the little beauty. So tell already. It was a nice sad story?"

Mama made herself comfortable as she sat back in the chair and cradled the baby in her arms. Ike winked at Sammy and glanced at Bessie. Sammy caught on and he and Ike squeezed next to Bessie like two pieces of bread around a chunk of cheese.

Ike knew he had to speak before Bessie did. He hoped Mama wouldn't hear from his voice that something was wrong.

"So what is the story of *Broken Blossoms?*" Mama asked impatiently. "What kind of troubles did the poor girl have?" Mama pushed a hair out of Herbie's baby sister's eye and waited some more.

Bessie's words burst out. "Troubles! Boy, did we have troubles! Ow!" She turned to Sammy who had pinched her leg.

"The film broke, Mama, so we didn't see it all," Ike muttered quickly. How could he tell her he was so busy watching the fire door and the usher that, although he remembered something about the famous moviemaker D. W. Griffith filming just north of the Bronx and something about extras getting a dollar-fifty a day, he didn't even know what *Broken Blossoms* was about. *And,* if he told her the whole truth, he might get the other boys in trouble.

It didn't feel good not telling Mama the truth. But the thought of telling her the truth didn't feel good, either.

He hardly had a moment to think about it because just then Bessie blew her whistle at Sammy. Everyone was startled and the baby began to cry.

"*Oy!*" Mama clutched the baby. "What are you blowing, Bessie? What? And where did you get it?"

As Mama spoke, the whistle dropped out of Bessie's mouth.

"Mama . . ." Ike said, picking up the whistle from the linoleum floor whose flowers had vanished with a million scrubbings. "It's a whistle, Mama. A prize from inside the Cracker Jack."

"Inside the *what?*" Mama asked, handing the baby back to Herbie.

Ike wished he could shrink away and disappear like butter in hot cereal. Then he wouldn't have to decide what to do—to tell or not to tell—or worry that Bessie would tell first.

Mama sat down again, and the kitchen chair

squeaked, even though she was only four feet seven inches tall.

Ike wished he had a third choice because if telling the truth was right and not getting your friends in trouble was also right, there must be a third answer. But what? He looked at his scuffed-up shoes. Sometimes, like now, he wished he was little like Bessie and could lean up against Mama and feel safe; like nothing could be wrong, ever.

"Where did you get money for Cracker Jack, Bessie?" Mama asked.

All the boys were silent. They waited for Bessie to answer. Ike was sure she would tell about much more than Cracker Jack. He winked at Sammy and the two boys made a sandwich out of Bessie once again, standing tightly on either side of her. Then Ike started to answer while Bessie was busy avoiding another pinch.

He cracked his knuckles. Mama heard the sound and raised an eyebrow. She gently put her hand under his chin and lifted his face.

Ike looked into Mama's blue eyes. Then he knew the third choice . . . Trust. "So, Mama," he said. "I better tell you the sad story. Only it's not about a poor girl in trouble. It's about a boy named Ikey who is very dumb and stupid and bad and who did a dishonest thing, on the Sabbath, yet." And Ike explained how it was his idea to help his penniless friend, Herbie, sneak into the movie, "Only, before I knew it, my little dishonest idea grew like a crack grows in a cold glass when hot tea is poured into it," Ike said, "and five friends sneaked in. We were caught and had to run from the usher." Ike did not tell how Bessie had kicked the usher. "But I told him we'd pay back double next time," Ike added, hoping that would save him.

Mama listened to every word. She sighed. She drummed her fingers on the table. The boys all waited silently. Even Bessie and the baby seemed very quiet. For a long time, it seemed to Ike, Mama didn't say a word. Then . . . she got up from the chair slowly and beckoned with her fingers.

"Come with me, Ikey," Mama said walking into the bedroom.

The other boys gasped.

"She must be getting his Papa's strap," Morton said.

"Boy, is he gonna get it," Tony Golida said.

"It's all my fault," whispered Herbie.

In the next room, Mama closed the door and sat down on the bright, flowered comforter. She patted the bed, smoothing the blanket and telling Ike where to sit, next to her. Ike was ready to accept his pun-

ishment. He clutched the bedpost. "Go ahead and hit," he said, closing his eyes and tensing his muscles.

Mama spoke softly but sternly. "You should have known better, Ikey. You did do a stupid thing. But a person who helps a friend cannot be a terrible person."

Ike barely breathed.

"The worst trouble," Mama went on, "is when you call yourself stupid and dumb. It's like giving yourself a smack—with words. So why, Ikey? Why? If anyone is going to give you a smack, it will be me."

So . . . lightning did not strike Ikey, but Mama did.

Mama stood up, leaned over and swatted his backside. "And that's not because you're stupid," she said. "Because you're not stupid. And that's not because you're dumb or bad. Because you're not dumb or bad."

"So why did you hit me, Mama?" Ike asked in a very low voice.

"That's for sneaking into the movies," Mama said and she shook a finger at him. "So! To help Herbie by cheating the theater owner is not a true kindness. You're not to sneak again. You will grow up to be a somebody, not a sneak. And helping someone else sneak is sneaking yourself. If your friend needed money, you ask. I would give you from the *pushka,* you hear?" Mama pointed to the kitchen as if seeing the tin can of pennies.

"Yes, Mama," Ike said, his mind wandering to the newsreel and D. W. Griffith paying extras a dollar-fifty. A dollar and fifty cents must be a lot of pennies, Ike thought.

"And remember, Ikey, my kind, smart son, we all sometimes do things that are not so good. So we learn from them. So now you know better." Mama reached over and stroked Ike's curly hair.

"So, you said you will pay back double next time? That's a good boy. You tried to make it right. And you tried to help your friend. You are sounding like a good problem solver, a grown-up boy."

That's funny, Ike thought. Now it felt good and safe to be grown up.

"Come, Ikey," Mama said. "We must discuss the paying back double with your friends so they, too, will know how to help without doing a wrong thing. And I'm thirsty, Ikey, let's all have a glass of seltzer." And she led the way back to the kitchen where the boys sat slumped over the table waiting for a black-and-blue Ike.

But . . . Ike appeared in excellent spirits.

"Not a rip or a mark," said Danny, examining Ike in amazement.

"Bet you can't sit down!" said Robert, rubbing his own backside sympathetically.

"In this house," said Mama, "rugs are for beating. Children are for teaching. Now!" Mama got everyone's attention with a single word. She sprayed seltzer from the green bottle into glasses and put the bottle back in the icebox, as she spoke. "A special plan is needed. A where-to-earn-money-to-pay-back-the-theater-owner plan. He, too, has children to feed. This plan you must think of yourselves like you made the problem yourselves."

The boys looked guiltily at the floor. "We're sorry, Mrs. Greenberg," Danny Mantussi spoke for all the boys, "We didn't mean no harm."

Mama nodded, then left the room, taking Bessie and Herbie's baby sister with her.

Before the glasses were empty, Ike and his friends had come up with the best plan yet!

4. The Special Plan

Ike was up early Sunday morning. So was Mama. Later on, she would help Bessie dress and then take her down to the basement room where on Sundays and weekdays Mama was a businesswoman, selling cloth from boxes. "Piece goods," Mama called it. Bessie would play with scraps or snooze in a carton with Baby #4 tucked under her arm. She would suck her thumb, and with her other hand, feel the softness and warmth of a piece of red velvet, an odd piece Mama would cut up and sell for hair ribbons. But now, in the kitchen Mama was just Mama, dishing out Ike's breakfast.

After swallowing a mouthful of steaming porridge and feeling its warm path down his throat, Ike buckled his woolen knickers and raced to the window. He didn't hear any wind outside or any patter of rain on the glass and he was glad. The special plan depended on the weather.

Mama sliced a salami sandwich, wrapped it in a napkin and stuffed it in a brown bag with a grease spot already on it. The garlic smell of the kosher salami made Ike yearn for lunch.

"So," Mama said. "Today my Ikey has a secret plan to earn money? But north of the Bronx, you have to go? You can't deliver for the fruitman or sell extra newspapers?"

Last night, Papa, too, had said this to Ike. "To Mamaroneck you're going, to earn money? Someone there is going to reach out and say 'You want a job, Ikey Greenberg?' In a factory you earn money."

Ike began to worry. Maybe he wouldn't be allowed to go. Yesterday the boys had discussed and agreed upon a plan. But part of it had to be kept a secret. They would tell where they were going and that they were going to try to earn money; but they would not tell how. Because, IF they got to Mamaroneck, just north of the Bronx . . . IF they did get to be extras in D. W. Griffith's new silent movie, *Way Down East* . . . and IF any of them were really paid a dollar-fifty like the Pathé newsreel had said; then they would have a real surprise for their Mamas and Papas.

The boys planned to pay back the twenty-five cents, double money for the five boys they'd sneaked in at the movie house. But they would also have enough money to treat their Mamas and Papas. They would take them all to the movies instead of just telling them the story.

Just the thought of such a surprise made Ike feel like a bedspring ready to pop. And he might get to see a real movie camera, too! What a day! This was the best plan yet—if it worked! . . . If Mama didn't change her mind about letting him go. Ike was ready to leave this second.

"You will ride your bike carefully, Ikey, right?" Mama spoke seriously, one eyebrow raised. "You are sure you have to go so far? You will stop at corners and look both ways for horses and automobiles?" Mama was really telling rather than asking. As Ike put on his dark woolen jacket, Mama stopped talking a moment to scratch her back on the edge of the doorway. "*Ah mechaieh,*" she sighed—the relief of a conquered itch.

"Hurry, Mama," Ike said, reaching for the bag with his lunch in it.

"What a beautiful Sunday morning you have,"

Mama said. Then her smile disappeared. "But take your scarf anyway, Ikey. You never know. It could snow, even." Mama held her chin as if deep in thought.

It was going to happen. Any minute she'd say "Better not go."

Ike shifted his weight impatiently and sighed. "I'll take the scarf," he said. And to himself—Anything. Just let me go, he prayed.

Then, just when Ike thought he couldn't wait another minute, Mama said, "So go already. I'm in a hurry to sell my cloth. What are you waiting for?" But she still squeezed his shoulders. How could he go?

"Oy, Ikey," she said with a hug, "you are growing up." Mama smiled the biggest smile yet. Then she pointed a pudgy finger at him and said, "But be careful. You hear? At every light you remember my words. DON'T STOP SHORT. Broken bones even grown-up boys don't need!"

Ike knew that to Mama saying such words had the power of keeping anything bad from happening . . . of keeping him safe.

Mama turned Ike around, opened the door and with a swat at his backside, sent him on his way.

What freedom Ike felt as he flew down those steps,

two at a time, swinging around corners, hanging onto the banister, jumping the last three steps and landing with a bang so loud that Mrs. Mantussi opened her door and peeked out. Ike could smell bacon cooking—a smell that never came from his own apartment. One thing being kosher meant was not eating bacon, or any pork. That was one of the rules Mama would never bend.

"What took you so long?" Tony Golida called from the outside doorway as he held the door open for Ike. "I've even been to church already."

Ike dragged his half rust, half blue bike out from under the stairs and bumped it down the outside stone steps. What a perfect day this would be!

Morton Weinstein, James Higgins, Herbie and Joey, Robert, Patrick, Jack, Dave, Sammy, Danny, Tony, Bernie and Sol, who were all ready, watched as Ike stuffed his lunch into a leftover World War I canvas pack strapped to the back of his bike.

"My father drew the directions," Patrick said handing Ike a wrinkled piece of newspaper. "He said it doesn't take him long to ride there. We gotta take the Boston Post Road all the way." Mr. Murphy delivered furniture on a truck, so everyone in the neighborhood always asked him how to get anywhere.

Ike glanced at the black lines and stuffed the paper into his pocket.

Sammy kicked his tire, then got on his bike.

With a wave from Ike, who was in the lead position, the army of bike riders were on their way, pedaling up East 136th Street to the end of Brook Avenue, caps, hair and scarves flying in the breeze.

Without looking back, Ike knew Mama and Bessie were probably waving good-bye from the window. He wasn't going to Europe, he thought . . . just to Mamaroneck . . . just north of the Bronx. It couldn't be far.

The parade of bicycles whizzed past four-story apartment houses with bedding airing out on each fire escape. Past the firehouse, where Ike's friend the fire chief waved and Ike waved back. A jog right, and the boys were on 3rd Avenue. A few blocks more, another right turn, and they were on the Boston Post Road at last. It was a great day. Everything was going to be terrific. They were off to a nice easy start. There would be plenty of time to get to Mamaroneck by noon, stay a while and ride back before dark.

"We take the Boston Post Road all the way," Ike shouted.

Soon Ike saw Charlotte Street on the right and

Crotona Park up a block on the left. The cobbled pavement bumped under the bike wheels as Ike came to a stop. It wouldn't hurt to rest for a little while. There was plenty of time. One by one the other bikes stopped, and the boys gathered together to admire Charlotte Street's fine brick apartment houses with wrought-iron stair rails and carved granite cornices above.

"They got polished brass mailboxes, and marble in the halls like a castle," Ike said. "I know because Mama took Bessie and me, special, to a lady dentist in there, to see that ladies can be a somebody, too."

"A lady dentist?" Herbie Friedman said.

"She pulled my tooth," Ike answered rubbing his cheek. Then he waved. "Come on. Let's get going."

The army of fourteen boys continued pedaling out of the South Bronx. Up the Boston Post Road they went. On . . . and on . . . and on, riding through Bronx Park with its duck pond and cages of wild animals.

"I'm getting tired," Bernie whined. "Let's watch the bears at the zoo."

Of course they could stop for a while, to eat, rest and make plans, Ike figured. There was plenty of time to get to Mamaroneck. The boys quickly parked their bikes on the dirt path near the wooden arrow marked BEAR PITS. Patrick Murphy unwrapped a fish sandwich and read the Katzenjammer comics it was wrapped in.

Then the boys sat down on the hard March ground and munched, traded sandwiches and planned some more. The mixed smells of salami, sausage, cabbage and oranges filled the air. The bears growled hungrily from the zoo pits nearby.

Between bites, the boys discussed.

"I'm so tall and handsome that Griffith fellow will beg me to be in his picture," Danny said, putting his thumbs in his pockets and strutting around.

"You're so ugly you'll bust the camera," Sammy chuckled.

The word "camera" sent shivers of excitement up Ike's back. Oh, how he would love to see a real camera.

"Hey, Ike," Morton Weinstein adjusted his glasses as he looked at his pocket watch. "It's eleven o'clock."

Ike got up and brushed dirt from his pants. "Eleven o'clock. Let's get on our way." The time was going fast. But there was still an hour till noon. Mamaroneck couldn't be far. "We got plenty of time," Ike shouted.

The boys got up, threw a bite of sandwich to the bears and tossed their bags into the trash can. They wiped their mouths on their sleeves. Sammy burped as loud as he could . . . the others tried to burp louder, but couldn't.

The boys kicked up their U-shaped kickstands, mounted their bikes and rode on . . . and on . . . and on. Then a terrible thought crossed Ike's mind.

What if they only film in the morning? What if he and his friends were already too late. Maybe they shouldn't have stopped at Charlotte Street or the zoo. But they could still make it if they pedaled fast and didn't stop for anything else, Ike figured.

"Are we there yet, Ikey?" Joey shouted.

"It can't be far," Ike called back, his words trailing behind him to the thirteen bike riders who followed. "Shortly," he added. That's what Mama always told him on the endless train ride to Coney Island. Ike's legs ached from pedaling. Every now and then a cold gust of north wind pushed against his face. It seemed to be getting colder.

The scenery was changing now as the boys traveled north. No more cars or horses. No more fancy apartments, in fact, there were no apartments at all. No stores or schools or anything. Ike took a deep breath. The air smelled sweet. No cooking or garbage smells. No burning coal. They were in the country. Wide open fields. Cows and sheep relaxing on the crisp brown winter grass, mooed and baaed their greeting as the caravan of bikes passed.

The boys rode . . . and rode . . . and rode. Muscles aching. Bikes squeaking. Mamaroneck couldn't be much farther . . . or could it? Ike wondered. Would they collapse before they got there?

"I never knew the Bronx was so big," Ike shouted, then stopped and pulled Mr. Murphy's black-lined directions out of his pocket. The boys were happy to stop and rest their weary legs, but Ike was worried. It must be almost noon and there was not a second to spare. Ike smoothed out the wrinkled paper. It didn't *look* far, as a line drawn on paper. It only looked like an inch to Mamaroneck. Then Ike realized Mr. Murphy must have meant it wasn't a long ride by motor truck, not pedal bikes. "Hurry up you guys," Ike said, finally admitting there might be a problem. "We may be too late already."

"What do you mean?" Bernie and Sol asked.

But Ike did not stop to answer. For now there was yet another problem: Not only were they late, but now to make matters worse, the weather was definitely changing. A wind stirred the trees, and a cold feeling crept through the soles of Ike's scuffed-up shoes. The sun disappeared behind a very big, swollen cloud, a cloud that might be swollen with snow.

"Come on!" With these words, Ike, on his bicycle once again, led the others on their way north . . . and farther north. The wind got colder and colder, biting at their faces. The army pedaled under an El station, while a train roared overhead sending sparks flying down. Then over the bridge, with the bike wheels making a new sound on the other side, the boys rode out of the Bronx and into Pelham. Soon they saw the gentle hills of New Rochelle.

By now, thirteen voices called to Ike the worn-out words, "Are we there yet?"

"Soon," Ike answered. "Soon." But he, too, wondered when. The cloud above looked ready to burst. And Ike could no longer even feel his freezing toes.

As Ike and the boys entered the bustling village of New Rochelle, a trolley squealed along on its tracks, and the clanging bell sent the boys pedaling fast this way and that to get out of the way.

When they passed a big corner store with a sign that said BAUMER PIANO CO. VICTROLAS, the boys wanted to stop, rest and look at the window display. Ike, too, felt like stopping. His muscles felt ready to pop like a dried-out rubber band but he kept going.

Onward, through the gentle curves of Larchmont,

where huge picture-book mansions loomed.

And then, just as thirteen weak voices called, "When, Ikey? When, already?" Ike noticed tall marsh grasses in the field ahead, and the air tasted as salty as at Coney Island. He spotted a sign, and felt like the soldiers must have felt when they came home from the war, as he read: WELCOME TO MAMARONECK. "At last," he sighed.

A gull flew overhead and there it was . . . a glimpse of shoreline. ORIENTA POINT, the arrow directed. Ike looked around as he rode. There was another sign: THE GRIFFITH ESTATE.

"Hurray!" the boys shouted as they pedaled down the road toward the waterfront, in a last spurt of energy.

But, as they got to the flat open land and the big buildings, all was still. No whirring of a camera. No bustle of actresses and actors and crew. No anything.

Ike's heart sank. Were they too late?

Oh, no. Then he had the worst thought yet: It was Sunday. Maybe actors don't work on Sunday. Had he led his army all this way for nothing? No money? No being extras in the film? No surprise? For the first time, Ike was speechless. And to make matters worse, that cloud was overhead and the north wind sent a chill right through him, and a snowflake landed on tall Danny Mantussi's nose.

513

5. The Once-in-a-Lifetime Movie

Ike turned like the movie camera in the Pathé News, as he slowly looked around the Griffith Estate. He'd never seen such a big house before, and on so much land! Little bridges led from one building to another. The buildings had chimneys and towers like a picture-book castle he'd seen at the library.

"Look up there!" Ike shouted to everyone, pointing to a weather vane spinning wildly in the wind. "And there!" pointing to the stone seawall that curved along the water's edge.

The boys laid down their bikes behind the bushes and followed Ike as he raced down this path and up that one.

"That Griffith's got as many paths as the Bronx Gardens," Tony Golida shouted.

"Our whole block of apartments could fit on all this land," Ike said. "There's so much room." Then he pointed to the sweeping tree branches. "Look!" he yelled. "These tree branches are chained together."

"They got a tree thief around here?" Patrick Murphy asked.

"Must be because of the wind," Ike suggested, hanging on to his cap.

He kept the boys busy . . . so busy, he hoped they wouldn't notice the awful silence. The silence of plans that did not work out! The silence of no movie actors, no cameras, no scenery and no money. The boys tried the locked doors of one building and peered in the dark windows of another. The only sign of life Ike saw was a car way off in the distance.

Danny Mantussi was the first to say something.

"Some plans you make Ike!" Danny grumbled. "How are we gonna make money here? There's not even anyone to pay us! And how are we gonna get home in this snow? Huh?"

"Yeah," shouted Sammy. "We rode all this way for nothin'!"

Ike felt as if his mouth would never smile again. Not only were all the boys tired and cold but the snow was sticking to the ground. Ike wished he could disappear like Houdini. But Mama had taught Ike that, as bad as one moment is . . . the next one might be the best yet!

"So we learned something," Ike said, looking at the bright side. "We learned how big the Bronx is."

But the boys practically jumped on him.

"Learned, shmearned!" Sol shouted. The cold sea air turned his words into a trail of smoke, quickly covered by a flurry of snow. The boys stomped back behind the bushes to where they'd left their bikes.

Ike was saved only by the fact that with the flurry of snow there came a flurry of activity. In one building, dark window shades were pulled up and faces peered out. Suddenly, doors opened and cameras and crews seemed to come out of nowhere. Busy people, still buttoning their coats, poured out of the next building.

Ike signaled to the boys, who immediately forgot their fight, laid down their bikes again and followed him. They crept closer and closer, bending behind bushes until they were just three feet away from the activity.

Some of the busy people carried large sheets of paper and notebooks, clutched tightly so they wouldn't blow away in the wind. "Snow!" they shouted. "Snow! At last we can shoot the snow scene." Men wearing heavy overcoats, boots with clips on them and hats with ribbons around the middle came out carrying something big that rested on three tall, wooden legs.

Ike almost gave them all away with a shriek of joy when he saw what was sitting on the three tall wooden legs. It looked like three boxes sitting one on top of the other, with a big, thick rubber band stretched along the side. But Ike knew it was the Pathé movie camera. His heart beat with excitement. At least he'd gotten to see a real camera. One dream had come true.

He'd worry about getting home in this snow a little later. It couldn't hurt to watch for a little while. And maybe they could still be extras and earn a dollar-fifty each. That was a lot of money. A dollar and fifty cents could buy 600 pounds of potatoes, even, Ike figured. But what would make Mr. Griffith choose *them?* Ike wondered, waiting for an idea.

Morton Weinstein poked Ike and pointed, "Look at that beautiful lady," he gasped. "Isn't that the lady with the sad eyes. The one from the busted movie . . . *Busted Flowers?*"

"You mean Lillian Gish, the star of *Broken Blossoms?*" Ike had barely said the words when he realized Morton was right. It was Lillian Gish, and next to her, standing at the doorway, was a man Ike knew must be "a somebody of importance" because even Miss Gish listened to him, saying, "Yes, Boss."

Ike had never seen such clothes. The tall man wore a heavy camel coat with a thick belt with double holes in it and big cuffs. He had striped knit gloves on his hands, and he smoked a cigarette. His wide-brimmed hat, his nose and his finger all seemed to point in the same direction.

"That's gotta be Griffith," Ike whispered to James Higgins. Ike's mouth stayed open. He couldn't believe he was really seeing the famous Mr. Griffith from the Pathé newsreel, the man in charge, the man with the money . . . and Lillian Gish, yet, a real live movie star. Wow!

"Yeah," James answered, shivering with excitement as well as cold. He buttoned his top button.

"Shoot it, Billy!" Griffith spoke to the cameraman through a megaphone, and Ike and the boys jumped at the loud sound.

"What the heck is that?" Bernie grumbled. "It looks like a witch's hat with a hole at the point."

Ike looked at the megaphone, then his attention turned again to the camera and he listened to its comforting whirring sound.

"Build a fire, Billy," Mr. Griffith shouted. "Build it under the camera so the oil in the camera doesn't freeze."

And Billy listened, yelling, "Yes, Boss."

Everyone listened to Mr. Griffith.

Then, Ike noticed that other people had walked from that distant car he'd seen and now stood near the camera. But they were not filming and they were not acting. They, too, were watching, and there were kids among them.

"Hey, guys," Ike said, pointing to some other boys. "Looks like we're not the only ones who want to be extras. How are we gonna get Mr. Griffith to ask *us?*" Putting the problem into words made Ike think of an answer. "Let's help that man, Billy, build the fire." So they politely offered to help. But still, no one asked them to be extras.

A man on the crew clapped a piece of wood on top of a slate and said, "TAKE NUMBER ONE."

Miss Gish was already standing at the side of a building which was painted to look like a general store. She had a dark cape wrapped around her and a kind of stocking cap on her head. And she carried a basket.

"Silence!" Mr. Griffith's voice bellowed through the megaphone, "Not even a word!" he added, pointing his finger at the onlookers, then touching it to his lips.

Ike thought the way he said that sounded like Mama. So he was sure everyone would listen. And they did . . . all except Morton Weinstein who thought he was whispering to Ike.

"If we hang around, maybe they'll play a love scene," Morton said.

Dave poked Morton in the ribs with his elbow. "And maybe you'll be in it," Dave said. Sammy made a kissing noise.

Mr. Griffith did notice the boys, but he did not ask them to be extras. He asked them to be quiet. Then he smiled and waved at the other onlookers as if he knew them. They waved back.

Ike figured he and his friends didn't have a chance to be extras. Mr. Griffith would surely choose the people he knew. He shivered and took out the scarf Mama had stuffed in his pocket. He wrapped it around his neck, waiting for an idea.

Behind Ike, the trees struggled with the wind, and the chains that held them rattled and pulled taut. Ike could see his footprints in the snow, and worry about the ride home zigzagged through him. But this was so interesting. Just a little while longer wouldn't matter.

"Now!" Mr. Griffith got everyone's attention with one word . . . just like Mama, Ike thought. "In the next scene, remember Miss Gish, you're shopping for the barn dance party. MEES GEESH, do you hear me?" Mr. Griffith joked with her name. "Swing your basket," he instructed, "and walk like a young girl. Hop around."

"Young girls don't do that," Miss Gish said.

"How else can I get the contrast between you and older people if you don't jump around like a frisky puppy?" Mr. Griffith answered.

Then Ike and Tony and Morton and James and all the other boys couldn't believe their eyes . . . Mr. Griffith, this big, tall, somebody, hopped around shaking his head as if he had curls. Ike wasn't sure who got the idea first, but one by one the boys all hopped around shaking their heads like Mr. Griffith, hoping he would see how well they'd listened and what good actors they were. Then he'd choose them for extras for sure.

But Mr. Griffith didn't notice. He was busy watching Lillian Gish. "That's a DARB!" he said, and laughed, raising his arm and making a circular O.K. sign with his thumb and finger.

"What's a darb?" Danny whispered to Ike.

"Sounds like a part from a chicken," Ike muttered.

"It must mean something is O.K.," Morton added. "Look at Mr. Griffith's fingers."

"It must mean something is even better than O.K.," Ike said. "Look at his smile. To me this snow is a darb!" he added, enjoying the word as he lifted a handful of snow and licked it, wishing he had syrup to pour over it. The snow felt good and tasted so clean. This was going to be a real snow. They hadn't had one all winter. They hadn't had a single snowball fight either. As they watched the cameras and the actors, Ike made a snowball, but he didn't throw it. He put it down next to him. The snow was getting deep very fast, he noticed. How would they get home? But he decided they would stay just a little longer.

Then Mr. Griffith was pointing at him. "What's your name?" he said to Ike.

Ike coughed to clear his throat. "Ike Greenberg," he said.

"Well, Ike Greenberg . . . You want to earn some money?"

Ike almost choked with excitement. This was the big moment. They'd be extras for sure. Then Ike laughed as he remembered Papa's voice saying the same words. "Someone is going to reach out and say 'You want a job, Ikey Greenberg?' In a factory you earn money." He couldn't believe it. For once, Papa was wrong.

"Yes," Ike said, looking up at Mr. Griffith, "I'd like to earn money." Then he looked at his friends.

"Come here," Mr. Griffith said, starting to walk.

He didn't stop walking, so Ike walked fast to catch up with him. Ike's heart thumped. He wanted to ask Mr. Griffith if the other boys could be in the movie, too, but what if Mr. Griffith got mad? Finally Ike got the words out nice and loud. "Can my friends earn money, too, Mr. Griffith?" he said, feeling very brave—and very generous at including his friends as extras in the movie. He was sure Mr. Griffith had seen them walking with a hop and had liked how they'd acted, too.

"Of course they can help," Mr. Griffith said. He looked up at the sky and said, "Looks like there will be a lot to do."

Ike couldn't understand what the sky had to do with it, but he was very happy as he called his friends. The boys crowded around and Ike told them the good news. They slapped him on the back, their way of thanking him for including them.

Then, Mr. Griffith signaled to his crew, and much to Ike's surprise there were . . . no cameras . . . no action . . . just three men handing out shovels to Ike and his friends as Mr. Griffith shouted to the boys, "Clear a path so we can put the camera on the platform with wheels. I'll pay you each a nickel." Then he yelled, "Billy! Move in! Get that face on Miss Lillian! Get that snow on her lashes. Real tears now, Miss Gish—for the sad scene before the ice floe. You can't make viewers cry with make-believe tears! Don't act it . . . Feel it!"

"Shovels!" Danny Mantussi muttered giving Ike a dirty look. "We rode all the way to Mamaroneck to shovel snow?" This time Danny didn't give Ike a thank-you slap on the shoulders. He gave him a swat!

Ike felt terrible. He was sure he'd figured out how to get to be an extra. "Well, anyway, we'll still earn money," he said, looking on the brighter side. "Five cents is not a dollar-fifty but it's something." That's all he could think of to say. He felt so disappointed. Shoveling they could do on East 136th Street. The sanitation department always hired them to shovel the snow down the manholes so the streets would be clear for traffic. And they paid a lot of money—twenty-five cents an hour.

Ike pushed the shovel in. This was not what the boys had dreamed they'd be doing in the first big snow. They'd waited all winter to have the East 136th Street snowball fight. A lump the size of a snowball grew in Ike's stomach as he and the boys shoveled the path clean. He ached to bend down, put the shovel aside and take a handful of that glistening white miracle and make the most perfect snowball. He forced himself to finish the job. But after the last shovelful, unable to stop himself, Ike dropped the shovel, grabbed a handful of snow, rolled it, patted it and then—as if the snowball had a mind of its own—it flew out of his hand and zoomed right at tall Danny Mantussi, always the first target in the East 136th Street snowball fight because . . . well, how could anyone miss such a big target?

Okay, so they wouldn't be in the movies, Ike thought, but they wouldn't miss the fun of the first snowball fight. At least they would have a good time.

Before anyone knew what was happening, snowballs were flying left and right. Sammy threw one at Ike, and as it slithered down his neck, Ike shivered and pulled his scarf tighter. Tony Golida's black jacket had white marks all over the back, where snowballs hit as he hid his face. Morton was screaming his usual, "Watch out for my glasses," and James Higgins threw the biggest snowball of them all.

The boys were too busy to notice the whirr of the movie camera and Mr. Griffith shouting orders. "Billy, don't miss the kid with the snow down his neck. Quick! Get the kid with the glasses. Get them all, Billy. That's it! Get them all. What a darb! What an absolute DARB of a snowball-fight scene!"

Finally the boys were satisfied and snow covered. They looked up.

"Now that's what I call acting!" Mr. Griffith said. "Here's a dollar-fifty for each of you." He reached into his pocket and paid each very snow-covered and surprised boy. Then he gave them each another nickel for shoveling.

At first Ike was speechless. He'd never seen so much money! The boys yelled "Thanks" and patted Ike on the back, a friendly pat. "What a good idea you had, Ikey," they yelled.

"See, I told you I'd think of something," Ike said, and he looked up at the sky, through the snowflakes and waved to someone higher.

6. The Long Wait

The boys jumped up and down in the snow yelling, "We're in the movies! We're stars!" And James Higgins felt the dollar bill between his thumb and middle fingers the way Mama always felt cloth. "We're rich!" he yelled. "We can take all our folks to the movies and our brothers and sisters, too!"

"We'll fill up the whole theater," Ike added. "And wait until the usher sees all of us paying customers." Then he looked around at the piled-up snow . . . "If we ever get home."

He wanted to stay some more to watch the camera and all, but he knew this snow meant business. After all, it had been saved in that cloud up there for three months.

"We better get on our way," he shouted.

"Let's break—a short break," Mr. Griffith bellowed through the megaphone. "I'm hungry! Let's eat," he said. "And Miss Gish, pull your cape tightly closed . . . I'm cold."

Ike wondered if he was thinking of Mama waiting and worrying at home or did Mr. Griffith really talk just like her.

Then Mr. Griffith thanked the boys and asked them where they were from and how they would get home in this blizzard.

"We rode our bikes here from East 136th Street in the South Bronx," Ike answered proudly. "You oughta make your movies over there. Then you'd have all the extras you want. On our block we're all extras. Like my Papa says—extra mouths to feed."

Mr. Griffith laughed, patted Ike's head and said, "Film on the city streets. I just might do that. So warm up by that fire before your long ride home," he added, "I'm cold. Hey, Joe," he yelled to one of the crew. "These kids will have a hard time riding their bikes in the snow. Give them the leftover chains, the kind we used to keep the branches on the old trees from breaking in the winter wind."

Ike was glad to hear why the trees' branches were chained.

"We'll strap the chains on their bikes," Mr. Griffith explained. "That will get them through the snow . . . if they walk their bikes up the hills. Get home quick as you can, boys. This snow means business!"

With the help of the film crew, including Mr. Griffith himself, Billy and even Miss Gish, the boys lifted their bikes out of the snow and dried them with rags, whispering to each other about the fact that they were rubbing shoulders with stars. The chains were put on the bikes, and after the boys warmed by the fire, Sammy sneaked over and kissed Miss Gish on the cheek. The boys all whistled and James Higgins yelled, in a singsong voice, "Sammy kissed a movie star." Sammy just sighed.

As the boys rode off, Ike yelled, "Mr. Griffith! When will the movie be in the South Bronx?"

They couldn't believe the answer.

"The movie's called *Way Down East,* and it will probably be shown there . . ." he stopped to think. "In July," Mr. Griffith shouted through the megaphone, and waved.

"In July" echoed in the air as the boys rode off, bumping along on the chains. He might as well have said next year! The boys could wait a week or even

a month, but until July? Four months? Ike wished time could move as quickly as in a movie.

The boys left Mamaroneck at two o'clock. If all went well they'd be home before dark, since they didn't plan to stop and eat at the zoo or sightsee as they'd done this morning. But although they pedaled harder, the bikes moved slower as the snow got deeper and deeper. And the cold they'd felt earlier now seemed like just a slight chill as they shivered back through New Rochelle. By the time they passed the Bronx Zoo they felt frozen, and hail hit against their cheeks like biting horseflies. But the real trouble struck just before they passed Charlotte Street, when Sammy yelled the worst news yet.

"I got a flat tire," he announced.

The boys had to stop to help Sammy fix his flat. Although they were happy to rest their weary, cold-stiffened legs, Ike was worried. It was getting dark and the snow was getting deeper by the minute. It must be almost four o'clock—or later—and Mama would surely be looking out the window for him and worrying.

It was hard enough to fix a tire without chains blocking the puncture, but to remove the chains when your fingers were frozen was even harder. The chains pressed against Ike's skin leaving pushed-in marks as he helped his cousin remove the hard metal and straps. Then Sammy pulled the air pump from the side of the bike and took a black rubber plug from his pocket. The snowflakes seemed to grow with each passing minute, and daylight was vanishing under a blanket of snow.

At last the tire was fixed, but although they tried this way and that, not one of the boys could get the chain to stay on.

"We'll just have to leave the chain and hope for the best," Ike said, using some of Mama's words to soothe his impatience.

The army of fourteen boys rode on, reminding Ike of his history lessons. Now he knew how Washington's men must have felt crossing the frozen, snow-covered Delaware River with blistering, bleeding bare feet. At least we have shoes, Ike said to himself as he led his exhausted troops past Crotona Park, feeling as if they'd never get home.

It was at the very last glimmer of daylight that they arrived, frozen, tired and hungry. Mama opened the door before Ike even reached the top of the stairs. With one hand on her heart, she moaned, "Oy, I was so worried with this snow. Where were you? It's almost dark already."

Ike melted like a snowman into his Mama's arms

and mumbled answers to her questions while begging to go to sleep. Whenever Mama said, "What did you say? What?" Ike soothed her with the words, "We're all fine. A wonderful day. A little late. I had to help Sammy fix his tire."

And as Ike collapsed into his bed, too tired even for dinner, he wondered how he and the other boys would ever save the money for the big surprise—save it until July, yet.

On Monday, the radio people talked about the blizzard—the eight-foot drifts of snow, and that crazy Mr. Griffith, filming in Mamaroneck. Ike heard it on his crystal radio set, the one he'd built last summer. Mama heard it too; they were in the kitchen, listening through the earphones. Mama warmed her hands on a glass of hot tea. The wind whistled through the cracks around the window, puffing up the white curtains.

"*Messhugge,*" she muttered. "In the snow they make movies? What craziness! Pneumonia they'll get."

Ike swallowed hard to keep the words from pouring out. He wanted to say, I was there, Mama, filming in the snow. It's not crazy. It makes the movie seem real. You'll see. I'll take you. But . . . he didn't say that. He cleared his throat instead and sipped his own tea.

Mama never asked if Ike earned the money or if he'd paid his debt at the movie theater. She'd said all she was going to say on the matter.

Of course, the boys all talked about nothing else. Until the next Saturday matinee at the Osceola Theatre when, along with their ticket money, they gave the woman in the box office an envelope marked: TO THE THEATER OWNER.

Inside was the money they owed, paid back double, and a note, carefully written by Morton Weinstein with just a little help with a word or two from his brother-in-law, Arnold, the high school graduate.

> DEAR THEATER OWNER,
> WE WILL NOT SNEAK IN AGAIN.
> CORDIALLY YOURS,
> THE EAST 136TH STREET PATRONS

They wanted to wave the extra dollar bills proudly. But people would wonder and talk and give away the secret . . . so they didn't.

The late winter seemed to build a snow fortress to keep out Spring. The boys whizzed down the hill at Brown Place and East 136th Street, on garbage can covers, stopping their dented sleds on the ashes the garbage collectors sprinkled at the bottom of the hill. They thought about the beautiful sled they could buy with the movie money. But they didn't buy it. They worried if they could keep themselves from spending the money until July. Instead of months away, July seemed like years away.

Once, in April, when Mama yelled at Ike for not sharing a chicken foot with Bessie, he almost told her. "How can you yell at a boy who is going to take you and Papa and Bessie to the movies? How can you yell at a son with such a surprise?" he nearly said. . . . But he didn't. He just bit his tongue to keep it from wagging.

In May, the money burned a slight hole in the boys' pockets and they decided to spend just a penny each . . . to tide them over. With noses pressed and flattened to the candy store's glass window, they made the difficult choice. Ike and Herbie selected hardtacks to suck on because they last so long. Sammy and Joey each spent their penny on rock candy and Morton and James wisely bought a roll of colorful sugar buttons because they'd last until July. Robert, Patrick and Jack Murphy bought licorice sticks because these were three for a penny, so they could buy three times as much. But Tony, Danny, Dave, Bernie and Sol made everyone else's mouth water when they went next door and each bought a sour pickle from the barrel. Garlic juice ran down their arms as they took bites.

All through June the money seemed to get as sticky as the weather, and they almost spent it on ice cream cones and a trip to Coney Island to go on the rides. . . . But they didn't.

Finally, July came and with it a breathless, sweating Ike, running like the gas-lamp lighter from house to house with the long awaited announcement.

"*Way Down East* is playing tonight! At the outdoor movie, in the alley at the Osceola Theatre! Tonight is the night of the big surprise!"

7. The Big Surprise

Ike could imagine Mama and Papa and Bessie's surprise as, hearing his father call from the window, he raced home for dinner. He knew he'd better get upstairs before the last echo of his father's voice or he'd get "what for." But Ike's heart was bursting with joy. It seemed as though it was more fun to surprise someone else than to be surprised himself. He tingled with excitement. He could picture Mama's sparkling eyes and Papa's crushing hug of thanks. His cheek already hurt from imagining the pinch Mama would give it.

The boys planned to let the surprise out a little at a time. In almost every apartment on East 136th

Street and Brook Avenue, the same conversation was going on at the dinner table. Ike was so excited that he couldn't even swallow the cool borscht, so soothing on a hot summer night. He just stirred the sour cream into the beet soup, enjoying the beautiful pink color.

"Mama, Papa, Bessie, I have a surprise for you," he said at last.

Papa didn't stop slurping the soup, and a speck of sour cream clung to his mustache.

Bessie never stopped guessing. "A ring, Ikey? A bicycle, Ikey? A ring, Ikey? A dress? A cookie? A ring?"

Mama didn't stop offering more borscht with sour cream to the family, making a scraping noise with the spoon on the bottom of the big pot.

"A good surprise I'll listen to," she said finally, sitting down. "A bad surprise you tell later so it shouldn't spoil the meal."

Ike jumped up, shaking the table. "A good surprise, Mama—a wonderful treat." Ike was enjoying the suspense. "The best surprise in the world . . . for the whole family, yet; for the whole block, even."

"What, Ikey, what already?" Mama said.

Bessie jumped up and down, and even Papa put down his soup spoon.

"Tonight I am taking you all"— and he paused

for effect until Mama and Papa were on the edge of their seats—"tonight I am taking you all to the outdoor movies at the Osceola Theatre. I am buying all the tickets myself. We will be paying customers," he said with importance. "A nickel a ticket. Not even a twofer bargain rate. No one will have to tell you the story, Mama. You will see for yourself a movie called *Way Down East.* The whole block is going."

That was all Ike said to his family, or Herbie or Patrick or Tony or Danny or the rest of the boys said to theirs. No one said a word about being *in* the picture.

"It rained nickels?" Papa asked.

"*Sha,* Papa," Mama said. "Ikey must have worked hard for so much money. You don't get a something for nothing!"

All Ike could think, while Mama pinched his cheek, was that a snowball fight was not hard work at all. It was fun. Was that a something for nothing, to earn money and have fun, too? Maybe Mama, too, was not always right.

Soon the entire neighborhood seemed to be emptying into the street. Families of different sizes and shapes all shouted greetings to one another. Like a wave on the beach at Coney Island they all floated down East 136th Street, past the grocery store, the

Chinese laundry and the butcher shop. Herbie pushed his sister's baby carriage and Bessie dragged her cigar box with her Baby #4 bumping along in it.

Tonight, the entire East 136th Street "army" and their families marched to the ticket booth of the Osceola Theatre. The boys pulled out their dollar bills and paid five cents for each family member's ticket. Ike even paid for Bessie to have a seat of her own, and still there was plenty of money left over for each boy to buy treats.

On this steaming, breathless night, the boys did not have to sit crowded together, peering down from Herbie Friedman's fire escape to watch the outdoor movie. Having earned a dollar-fifty each plus shoveling money, tonight, as paying customers, they all went inside the theater where the usher, flashlight in hand, opened the fire door and held it open for Ike and his friends as they proudly led their families through the doorway, to the outdoor theater. In this fenced-in alley, on clear summer nights, green wooden benches were lined up in rows with the screen and piano in front.

"May we have our fans, please?" Ike asked the usher. It seemed strange to talk to him instead of run from him, like the time they'd sneaked into this very same movie house or the summer night the boys peeked through the fence's knotholes until the usher threw sand from the other side. And Ike was very glad Bessie did not kick the usher like last time.

Tonight he felt like a somebody as he watched the usher give his family and friends each a round paper fan on a stick, a fan that advertised the cola drink called Moxie. As everyone fanned the hot air and buzzing mosquitoes, they waited until it was so dark you could see only an occasional flicker of a fire fly and the stars winking above.

Finally the movie started, with lists of names and captions with some words even Ike could not read. Then, there was Lillian Gish as Anna, a country girl who, in need of money, was sent by her mother to ask rich city relatives for help.

"She falls in love with a handsome villain." Ike whispered the captions to Mama, Papa and Bessie.

Every now and then the boys would poke each other and whisper, waiting for the moment of the biggest surprise of all. Their moment on the screen. Their snowball fight.

The piano player next to the screen played dadada-dum at the parts where the villain appeared, and when Anna, played by Lillian Gish, held her sick baby in her arms, Ike saw tears streaming down

Mama's cheeks and even Papa sniffled and wiped his eyes. Bessie hugged her Baby #4 tightly.

But still there was no snowball scene. Had Mr. Griffith forgotten to put it in? Maybe it hadn't come out well. Ike worried.

At intermission the candy butcher walked around and the boys bought bonbons and ice cream and popcorn for everyone. Tony Golida's brother even found a tin watch in his bonbon box. Ike could not sit still. In his excitement, he bought box after box of Cracker Jack, never eating a one. Frantically, he searched for the prize, but he didn't keep it. He put the whistle or earring back in the box, then gave the box to a friend.

Mama watched Ike strangely. "What are you, a Cracker Jack inspector? What!" She said to Ike. "And still you have so much money?" She flicked her fingers at him and raised her eyebrow.

But Ike continued buying Cracker Jack until finally he reached into the last box, pulled out a prize, put that prize in his pocket and sat down.

The movie was on again and each boy glanced at the others, waiting for the snow scene to start. They waited, and waited . . . and waited. Tony coughed a signal at Ike that said, "When?" Ike shrugged his shoulders, signaling back that he didn't know. Popcorn smells filled the air. And the juice from a chocolate-covered cherry made Ike's fingers stick together. Sammy swatted at a buzzing mosquito. It happened to be on Sol's sister Becky's head. She swatted back.

Still no snow scene. On the screen, Lillian Gish as Anna walked down a dusty road. And the piano player's fingers walked slowly over the keys.

"Oy," Mama moaned as if she'd walked as far and was as tired as Anna.

Then, Ike's heart pounded as snowflakes fell on the screen and the boys recognized the background of the Griffith Estate and the painted general store. Every boy poked his Mama and Papa. "Watch this! Watch! This is really good!"

There was Anna in her black cape, carrying her basket. And there it was. Bigger than life. The screen burst into action. Snowballs flying. The audience, too, became busy. Then came the close-up!

The first thing Ike heard was his Aunt Sadie yelling, "Sam! Get off that screen!" Then she jumped to see Sammy still sitting next to her.

Ike didn't know where to look. He wanted to see himself on the screen and he wanted to see the look on Mama's and Papa's faces.

Mrs. Mantussi called out to the Danny on the

screen. "No gloves? Your fingers will freeze. Making snowball's with bare hands?"

And poor Morton Weinstein. His mother sneezed and missed the whole scene. She kept saying, "What? What happened? What?"

The boys clapped and cheered at themselves. And Bessie whispered to Baby #4 proudly, "That's my brother . . . mine!"

Mama sat up straight and grabbed Papa's arm. Then Papa spoke. He cleared his throat, leaned forward in his seat and said, "What the hell is going on?" Papa covered his mouth to pull back the word that had popped out. He smiled and pounded Ike's back. Then he hugged and kissed Ike. Papa's mustache tickled Ike's nose. "A regular somebody, my son. A big shot movie star, even." Papa muttered.

But Mama didn't say a word. Not one. She stared at the screen. Why didn't Mama hug and kiss him? Ike wondered. Didn't she notice he was in the movie? Maybe she had so many tears in her eyes that the faces were all blurred and she hadn't recognized him.

Ike wished Mama would say something. He even wished she would pinch his cheek or say "Don't eat any more candy, Ikey, my stomach hurts." But all Mama did was cry, watch the movie and cry. Ike thought a terrible thought. Maybe Mama had noticed him but was angry. Maybe she thought he'd sneaked into the filming of the movie. Ike worried. Maybe he was even going to be in trouble.

Mama watched poor Anna stranded on the dangerous ice floe and she gasped and cried until the movie was over and Anna was safe and happy. Then she wiped away a tear and took Ike's chin in her hand. Finally, Mama spoke.

"Now that's a movie picture!" she said. "It's so good it can make you cry on a happy day like this." Then she kissed Ike's forehead and said, "Thank you, Ikey dear. Thank you for taking me to see such a picture." Before Ike could speak she added, "It's easy to cry at a picture when you're already sad. But to make you cry when you're happy . . . *nu!* That's a picture!"

Ike was glad Mama enjoyed the movie, but when would she say that she saw him in it? Everyone was walking out of the theater already. And still Mama hadn't said what Ike wanted to hear.

Finally, as the neighbors crowded together on the street, Mama put her arm around Ike. Mama wiped away another tear from her eye and pinched Ike's cheek until it was red.

"And!" she said, getting everyone's attention.

OSCEOLA

Ike listened. Now would she say she saw him acting in the movie? He couldn't wait much longer.

Mama put her hands on Ike's shoulders and spoke loudly. "The best actor is right here with me," she said. "So tell me, Ikey dear. How did you do it, this wonderful surprise? How did you get in the movies? And how did you have money for all this?" Mama waved her hand around.

Everyone seemed to listen for Ike's answer. He took his time, enjoying the moment he'd waited for. "Mama . . . It was in March." Ike began. "Remember the snowy day I got home late? I was with my friends in Mamaroneck, Mama, just north of the Bronx. We rode our bikes to where this movie was being made. And I saw a real camera, Mama, and D. W. Griffith himself. And Mama, I saw movie stars—Miss Gish even." Ike couldn't hold back a laugh. "We not only got into a movie without paying . . . *WE* got paid. A dollar-fifty for being extras."

Mama put her hands on her own cheeks and chuckled. "America *gonif,*" she said out loud.

Ike explained what Mama said to his friends. "Only in America, Mama says, only in America could such a thing happen."

Then Ike called Bessie. He even put his arm around her shoulders. "I have something special for you," he whispered, reaching into his pocket.

"What Ikey, what?" Bessie asked.

But before she could guess her usual wish, Ike reached into his pocket and pulled out the prize he'd saved from the last Cracker Jack box. Ike slipped the tin ring with the genuine fake diamond onto Bessie's little finger. Yes, he always felt happy when he gave Bessie a present. But today he was so happy that he even accepted her slurpy kiss on his cheek.

Then all the families seemed to be hugging or kissing or thanking the boys as they all left the front of the Osceola Theatre and marched merrily back to East 136th Street. Happy Mamas and Papas and brothers and sisters all following the leaders—the East 136th Street army of boys, movie stars, yet!

and actresses—even the famous actress Miss Lillian Gish in *Way Down East*—how to make the story come alive on the screen. D. W. Griffith was both producer and director—a true moviemaker.

According to Miss Gish, in her book *The Movies, Mr. Griffith and Me,* "That's a darb!" was one of Mr. Griffith's favorite expressions of pleasure when a scene was done well. And the tree branches really were chained to keep them from breaking off in the sweeping winds at Orienta Point, Mamaroneck.

Many scenes of the silent movie *Way Down East* were actually filmed at the Griffith Estate in Mamaroneck, New York, just north of the Bronx. Extras were really used in this movie, and, in 1976, Mamaroneck High School students videotaped interviews with some of the surviving extras for a bicentennial project.

In the New York Museum of Modern Art's film collection is a copy of *Way Down East* in which there is a snowball-throwing scene. It is also true that some children from the South Bronx would ride their bikes north, loving to watch the filming and dreaming of being extras.

So, even though *Ike and Mama and the Once-in-a-Lifetime Movie* is fiction, it is quite possible that Ike and his friends could have been the boys in the movie and it's fun to imagine that they were!

Afterword

Ike and Mama and the Once-in-a-Lifetime Movie is a fiction story based on researched facts. D. W. Griffith really was a famous American movie producer and director in the 1900s. He was called the father of American film.

A movie producer, as Ikey would say, is the person in charge of gathering money to pay for making the film. He is the boss, as Griffith was called by actors, actresses and cameramen, the person who guides the film from the production to the theater.

A movie director reads the script, sees the story in his or her mind, selects and teaches the actors